Celestino Piatti's Animal ABC

For Andreas Michael

Distributed in the United States by NorthSouth Books, Inc., New York 10016.
Library of Congress Cataloging-in-Publication Data is available.
ISBN: 978-0-7358-4206-9
Printed in Latvia by Livonia Print, Riga, January 2015
1 3 5 7 9 • 10 8 6 4 2
www.northsouth.com

Celestino Piatti's Animal ABC

Written by Hans Schumacher
Illustrated by Celestino Piatti
English text by Jon Reid

A

The alligator's
Tears will end
His toothache eased
By his good friend

B

The bees sting bears
With quite a buzz
But nothing's left
Where honey was

C

Chameleons
Wait in disguise
Then tongues fly out
At tasty flies

D

The dolphin plays
All day at sea
How nice to whirl
In seafoam glee

E

Wise elephant,
Who has no hands,
Will use his trunk
To meet demands

F

Down to water
Frog will jump—
Then there he is
Upon a stump

G

Longer than giants, oh taller than tall,
Giraffes munch on treetops and gaze over all

H

Hares in danger
Run and hide,
Which shows great sense
But little pride

I

Strange ibis flies
But when at rest
He likes a marsh
With fishes best

K

Tall kangaroo,
Who roams the wild,
Gives high-jump rides
To her small child

J

Who left the track
While others slept?
Across the page
A jaguar crept

L

The lion hears
The mouse's plea
And since he's small
Lets him go free

M

N

Sweet flutelike notes
In the spring night
'Tis nightingale
Makes such delight

Who's this who hangs
Yet takes no chances?
Orangutan!
He hides in branches

P

Dressed for dinner
Minding manners
Penguins flaunt their
Coattail banners

Q

To buy a quetzal bird
In a brilliant feather gown
Just spend a quetzal coin
In a Guatemalan town

R

Rhinoceros,
Old blunderbuss,
Your nose-horn scares
The best of us

S

Poor snail can't run
Away from home
Because she has
Her house in tow

T

When tiger growls
To be caressed
Just ask what he
Thinks tastiest

U

The Ural owl
His hoots advise
Is wise to those
In night's disguise

V

Vicuña has no hump
As cousin camels do
But shares with cousin llama
A mountain rendezvous

W

Whale grins and floats
And churns the sea
Then spouts a cup
Of salty tea

X

Xopiatti
Monster X—
Bird-fish-leopard—
How complex!

Y

Big shaggy yak
Gives milk and meat
Don't be afraid
Her temper's sweet

Z

When zebra wears
His stripes at night
The only ones
You see are white

"Feeling, craftsmanship and imagination were the highly concentrated ingredients of his life's work." —Bruno Weber

Celestino Piatti — Life and Work
Celestino Piatti was born in Wangen in 1922 and grew up in Dietlikon, near Zürich, Switzerland. He studied graphic art in Zürich from 1938 to 1942, and during this period produced his first drawings and watercolors. His very first poster (1948) won him an award, and many more followed, including the Golden Brush (1976) for the book covers he designed for DTV (Deutscher Taschenbuch Verlag). The owl motif appeared for the first time in 1952 on a poster advertising books. In addition to books and posters, Celestino Piatti designed postage stamps, stained glass, murals, ceramics, and sculptures; and he also worked as a cartoonist for the *Nebelspalter*. Although he used a wide variety of techniques, his style—black outlines and vivid colors—was always unmistakable. He died in 2007 in Duggingen, in the canton of Basel-Land, Switzerland.